It was a beautiful summer morning on the Island of

Sodor. The  was shining and the sky was

blue, without a sign of clouds.

 had just arrived at the station by the

sea. His passengers climbed out of the

and made their way to the beach. The children ran

on ahead. Some took off their  and got

ready to splash in the sea.

One of the passengers remained behind. He walked

along the platform to thank  for a

pleasant ride.

"Our pleasure, sir," said the driver. "Enjoy your day."

"Thank you," said the  . "I've bought a

new  and I'm taking a trip out in the bay

today. I might try to catch some  , too.

Good-bye, Thomas."

 wanted to stay and watch the boats at

sea and the children making , but

he had to return and collect some more passengers

instead. The conductor blew his  and

waved his green , and Thomas chugged

sadly back along the line.

Later in the morning, the weather changed.

Black  filled the sky and the wind blew

fiercely. Thomas struggled back to the station by the

When at last  pulled up to the platform,

the rain was pouring down and people were running

from the  to find shelter from the storm.

They were carrying beach towels and picnic bags,

 and .

One family took shelter under a  .

Others put up  . A clever man had

folded his newspaper and made himself a  .

The lucky ones had jackets. Soon the beach was

empty. The café filled up with people asking for hot

 and cakes.

 saw the lifeguard hauling up the danger

flag to warn people not to take out  or

swim in the sea. The lifeboat men stood by in

their yellow  and black boots.

Thomas looked out to sea. He hoped all the

 were out of the water and safe from

the storm.

Just then, Thomas noticed a little

bobbing in the bay. Suddenly, a huge wave hit it—and

the boat capsized! At once,  blew his

whistle loudly. His driver looked out of the

and people crowded around to see what was wrong.

Someone went to call the  to tell him that

the boat was in trouble.

 was worried that the lifeboat wouldn't

be able to reach the little rowboat in such a

rough sea. Then the message came that the station's

 was out of order. Thomas's driver knew

what to do. He told the fireman to put plenty of coal

on Thomas's  while he got permission to

take Thomas to the station by the airfield, where

 the Helicopter worked.

Then  hurried to the station by the

airfield, and his driver explained that a

 was in trouble out at sea. Soon the pilot

came and quickly took  up. The wind was

still blowing fiercely, but he was able to fly over the

 . Thomas arrived back just in time to see

the rescue in operation.

The helicopter crew lowered a harness, which was

attached to the , and slowly he was

hauled up to the helicopter.  then buzzed

away to the beach. The lifeboat, which had been

standing by, went back into the .

On shore, an  was waiting to take

the man to a hospital. The ambulance driver put a

blanket around the man and drove him away. At the

hospital, a  checked that he was all right.

Fortunately, he was just cold and frightened.

They gave him some dry clothes and some hot, sweet

 . Then a  came to take him home.

That night, in the engine shed, the engines chatted.

"Who would have thought beautiful

could change so quickly into a terrible storm like

that?" said  .

"It's lucky that Thomas saw that the boat was in

trouble," said  .

"Yes, well done, Thomas," said  .

"Your quick action probably saved the man's life."

The next morning,  had a visitor. It was

the rescued man who had thanked him for the ride.

"I've come to thank you again, Thomas," he said.

"The  was too rough to  in

yesterday. You and your driver were very clever to

raise the alarm."

Thomas whistled with pleasure.

Sir  was pleased, too.